A Little Princess Story

I Want A Sister!

Tony Ross

Andersen Press

"There's going to be someone new in our family,"
said the Queen.

"Oh goody!" said the Little Princess.
"We're going to get a dog."

"No we're not," said the King.
"We're going to have a new baby."

"Oh goody!" said the Little Princess.
"I want a sister!"

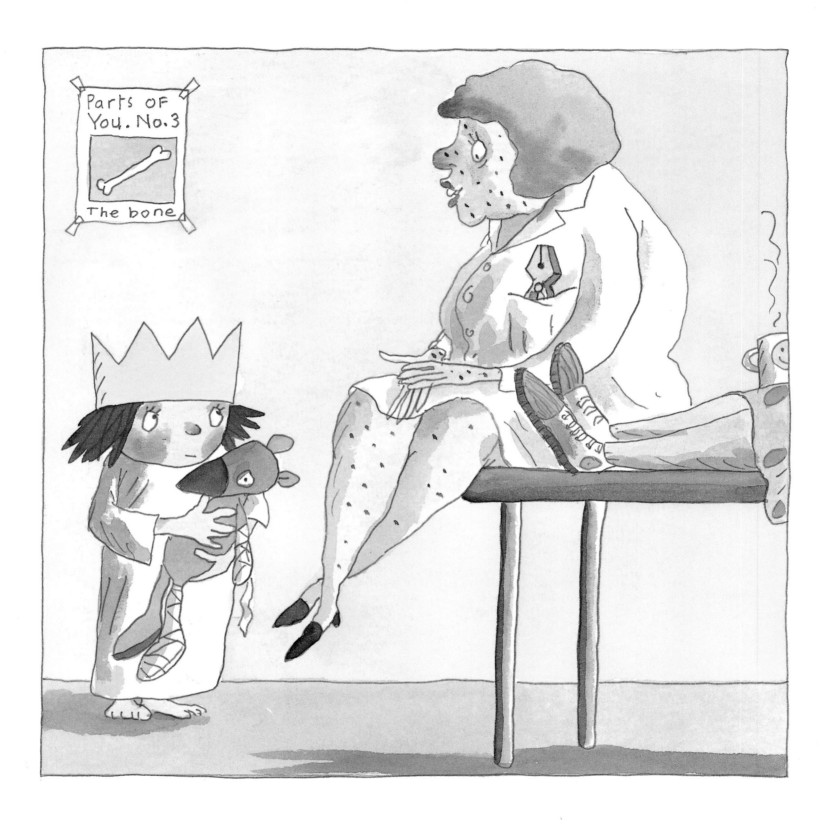

"It may be a brother," said the Doctor.
"You can't choose, you know."

"I don't want a brother," said the Little Princess.
"Brothers are smelly."

"So are sisters," said the Maid.
"Sometimes you smelled AWFUL."

"I don't want a brother," said the Little Princess.
"Brothers are rough."

"So are sisters," said the Admiral.
"Both make TERRIFIC sailors."

"I don't want a brother," said the Little Princess.
"Brothers have all the wrong toys."

"Brothers' toys can be just like yours,"
said the Prime Minister.

"Well," said the Little Princess,
"I JUST DON'T WANT A BROTHER."

"Why?" said everybody.
"BECAUSE I WANT A SISTER," said the Little Princess.

One day, the Queen went to the hospital
to have the new baby.
"Don't forget . . ." shouted the Little Princess,

". . . I WANT A SISTER!"

"What if it's a brother?" said her cousin.

"I'll put it in the dustbin," said the Little Princess.

When the Queen came home from hospital,
the King was carrying the new baby.

"Say 'hello' to the new baby," said the Queen.
"Isn't she lovely?" said the Little Princess.

"He isn't a she," said the King. "You have a brother.
A little Prince!"
"I don't want a little Prince," said the Little Princess.
"I want a little Princess."

"But we already have a BEAUTIFUL little Princess,"
said the King and Queen.
"WHO?" said the Little Princess.

"YOU!" said the King and Queen.

"Can my brother have this, now I'm grown up?"
said the Princess.

Other Little Princess Books

I Want My Potty! (board book)

I Want My Dinner! (board book)

I Want My Dummy! (board book)

I Want My Light On!

I Want My Present!

I Want a Friend!

I Want to Go Home!

I Want Two Birthdays!

LITTLE PRINCESS TV TIE-INS

Can I Keep It?

I Want My New Shoes!

I Don't Want a Cold!

I Want My Tent!

Fun in the Sun!

I Want to Do Magic!

I Want a Trumpet!

I Want My Sledge!

I Don't Like Salad!

I Don't Want to Comb My Hair!

I Want a Shop!

I Want to Go to the Fair!

I Want to Be a Cavegirl!

I Want to Be a Pirate!

I Want to Be Tall!

I Want My Puppets!

I Want My Sledge! Book and DVD